Candy Fairies

The Coconut Clue

HELEN PERELMAN

ILLUSTRATED BY
ERICA-JANE WATERS

ALADDIN
NEW YORK   LONDON   TORONTO   SYDNEY   NEW DELHI

This book is a work of fiction. Any references to historical events, real people, or real places are used fictitiously. Other names, characters, places, and events are products of the author's imagination, and any resemblance to actual events or places or persons, living or dead, is entirely coincidental.

ALADDIN

An imprint of Simon & Schuster Children's Publishing Division

1230 Avenue of the Americas, New York, NY 10020

First Aladdin paperback edition October 2015

Text copyright © 2015 by Helen Perelman Bernstein

Illustrations copyright © 2015 by Erica-Jane Waters

Also available in an Aladdin hardcover edition.

For information about special discounts for bulk purchases, please contact Simon & Schuster Special Sales at 1-866-506-1949 or business@simonandschuster.com.

The Simon & Schuster Speakers Bureau can bring authors to your live event. For more information or to book an event contact the Simon & Schuster Speakers Bureau at 1-866-248-3049 or visit our website at www.simonspeakers.com.

Book designed by Karina Granda

The text of this book was set in Baskerville Book.

Manufactured in the United States of America 0915 OFF

2 4 6 8 10 9 7 5 3 1

Library of Congress Control Number 2015942948

ISBN 978-1-4814-0617-8 (hc)

ISBN 978-1-4814-0616-1 (pbk)

ISBN 978-1-4814-0618-5 (eBook)

The Coconut Clue

To the supersweet students at
Seely Place Elementary!

Contents

CHAPTER 1

Lost Gummy Flavors

Raina the Gummy Fairy licked her lips. She was looking at a ripe orange gummy tulip. The flower was the most delicious color and shape. *"Sweet-tacular!"* she exclaimed.

Her basket was overflowing with freshly picked gummy flowers. "It's been a good season for these," she said to Blue Belle, her gummy bear friend. The bear nodded. Raina took good care of many animals in Gummy Forest. "Let's both have one," she said with a smile. The burst of orange flavor in her mouth made her grin.

"Hi, Raina!" Berry the Fruit Fairy called from above. "Hey, Blue Belle!"

"Berry!" Raina called. "You have to try these gummy tulips!"

Berry landed next to Raina. She was dressed in a beautiful purple-and-pink dress. Berry always dressed her best. She had all the fashion sense that Raina didn't have! No one could whip up an outfit like Berry.

Raina handed her a grape-flavored gummy tulip.

"Mmm, this *is* delicious," Berry said. "What

a great harvest! You should give some of these to Princess Lolli and Prince Scoop."

Raina had already given a bouquet to the ruling fairy princess and her husband. She loved visiting Princess Lolli and Prince Scoop at Candy Castle.

"I dropped off a basket of flowers for them yesterday," Raina told her. She reached into her bag. "Prince Scoop gave me this." She showed Berry a beautiful book with gold trim.

"Sweet sugars!" Berry exclaimed. "What is the book about?"

"The book is called *Tropical Treasures* and tells the flavor history of the Ice Cream Isles," Raina told her. "I was asking Prince Scoop about the different flavors of ice cream we ate at the Ice Cream Festival."

"Hmm," Berry said with a sigh. "Remember those tropical flavors like pineapple and coconut?" She rubbed her belly. "I sound like Dash, don't I?" She giggled.

Dash the Mint Fairy was their good friend. She was the smallest of their friends, but the one with the biggest appetite. She also always remembered every candy flavor she had ever had!

Raina opened the book. "Look at all these ice cream flavors," she said. She ran her finger down the list. "Mango, papaya, kiwi, pineapple, coconut . . . there are so many. And there's even a chapter about tropical-flavored gummy candies that once grew around Gummy Lagoon!"

"Gummy Lagoon?" Berry gasped. "No one

has been over there in ages. Do you think there is still candy there?"

A smile spread across Raina's face. "I'd like to be the Candy Fairy to find that out, wouldn't you?" she asked. She lifted her eyebrows. She knew that Berry would not be able to resist the idea of exploring a new place and looking for tropical-flavored gummy candies. "Let's ask the others at Sun Dip."

"I'm in," Berry said. "And I'm sure Dash will be up for an adventure." She grinned. "Especially if it involves a new candy."

"We might have to convince Melli and Cocoa," Raina said, thinking of her Caramel Fairy and Chocolate Fairy friends. "But that won't be too hard. I know they will want to help."

They both said good-bye to Blue Belle and flew off to Red Licorice Lake. Sun Dip was coming and their friends would be arriving soon. Raina put her fresh gummy flowers in a jar and placed the arrangement in the middle of the blanket.

"*So mint!*" Dash cried as she swooped down. "Those flowers look too perfect to eat!"

"Oh, I bet they are so juicy and delicious," Melli said. She flew in next to Dash.

Raina beamed with pride. "Try one," she said.

"Save one for me!" Cocoa called from above.

"Better hurry," Berry said, taking a red gummy daisy. "These are really good."

The five friends settled down on the blanket to eat the gummy flowers and watch the

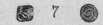

sun slowly sink past the tip of the Frosted Mountains.

Raina saw Berry looking at her. Berry was silently urging her to ask the others about coming with her to Gummy Lagoon. Raina took Prince Scoop's book out of her bag.

"Whoa!" Dash exclaimed. "Where'd you get that?"

"Prince Scoop lent it to me," Raina said. "It's called *Tropical Treasures*."

"It looks like a royal book," Melli added.

Raina nodded. "Prince Scoop let me borrow it. I was asking him about some of the flavors of ice cream in the Ice Cream Isles."

"Did you find out how to make some of those flavors?" Dash asked. She licked her lips. "Yum! They were delicious!"

"Actually, there used to be tropical-flavored gummy candies growing in Gummy Forest," Raina said.

"Pineapple, papaya, and mango gummy flowers?" Dash squealed. She shot straight up in the air.

Raina giggled. She knew Dash would get excited about new gummy flavors.

"Where?" Melli asked.

"Gummy Lagoon," Raina told her. She saw Melli's expression change.

"No one ever goes to Gummy Lagoon," Cocoa said before Melli could reply. "Isn't it haunted?"

Melli shuddered. "You don't plan on going there, do you?"

"Yes," Raina said. She looked over at Berry. "And I don't think it's haunted."

"Then why don't any of the Gummy Fairies go there?" Melli asked.

Raina shrugged. "I'm not sure, but I hope after reading this book I'll find out more," she said.

"There might even be different tropical flavors there," Berry said.

"We should check it out," Dash replied.

Raina opened the royal book. "I already read that some of the Ice Cream Fairies used flavors from the lagoon long ago.

"You mean you'll be able to grow gummies in the same flavors as those tropical ice cream flavors?" Dash asked. Her eyes were wide with excitement.

"Why hasn't any Gummy Fairy made tropical-flavored gummies?" Cocoa asked.

"Exactly," Raina said. "I want to find out why there are no gummies growing over by the lagoon anymore."

"You want to go to the haunted lagoon?" Melli asked nervously.

Raina leaned forward. "No one knows for sure if it's haunted. I don't think it is. Please

 11

come with me. Help me explore the lagoon and maybe find the flavors?"

Dash and Berry raised their hands high while Cocoa and Melli looked a bit worried.

"Are you *sure* it's safe?" Melli asked. Often she was the one to get the most nervous about adventures.

"Sure as sugar," Raina told her.

2

Tropical Treasure

The next morning, Raina waited for her four Candy Fairy friends at the edge of Gummy Lake. She was so excited to explore Gummy Lagoon. The area around the lagoon was not full of bright gummy candies like the rest of Gummy Forest. Maybe some Candy Fairies thought it was haunted, but after reading a couple of chapters in Prince Scoop's book Raina felt there might be some clue about what used to be there—and what possibly could still grow.

"Ready?" Cocoa asked as she flew down to Raina. Dash and Melli were right behind her.

"We're just waiting for Berry," Raina said, smiling.

"That's nothing new!" Dash exclaimed. "I am sure she is looking for just the right outfit for a tropical adventure."

Berry cleared her throat, and her friends looked up to see her flying above. "I am right on time," she declared. "You are all early!"

"Berry is right," Raina said. "I think every-one can't wait to see this lagoon."

 14

Melli wrapped her finger around her short dark hair. "Are you sure this is safe? Did you even ask Princess Lolli?"

Raina hadn't thought about asking Princess Lolli. It wasn't as if the lagoon was considered dangerous. She looked at Melli and sighed. "I think this visit is perfectly safe," she said. "We can always send a sugar fly to Candy Castle if we get into trouble."

"We won't get into any trouble," Berry said.

"We'll be heroes!" Dash exclaimed. "We're going to figure out what happened to the candy of Gummy Lagoon!"

Melli shrugged. "All right," she said. "But everyone needs to be careful."

"Sure as sugar," Raina replied.

"Did everyone bring supplies?" Dash asked.

Raina laughed. "You mean candy supplies, don't you?"

Dash blushed. "A Candy Fairy is always prepared. You never know when you will need a sweet snack. Now let's get going!"

The five fairies flew over Gummy Lake and up past Gummy Grove. Raina pointed to the left. "Over this way," she called.

From the sky, Raina could see where the bright colors of the gummy trees ended and the waters of the lagoon began. Her heart was beating so fast!

"Come this way," Raina said. She flew down to an area of white sugar sand near the murky lagoon.

"Holy peppermint!" Dash cried. "This lagoon doesn't look spooky and haunted. It

 17

just looks like all the color was washed away."

"If I were painting this scene," Cocoa said, spinning around, "I would only need gray and white paint."

Melli knelt down and touched the dry white sand. "This place is so sad."

"Be careful," Raina warned. "We have to be sure about the candy before we eat or touch anything."

Dash put her hands up in the air. "Don't look at me!" she said. "Fairy promise, I won't eat anything until you say so." Her eyes darted around at all the wilted vines of candy. "That might be the easiest promise ever!"

Raina laughed. "I know," she agreed.

"Something doesn't seem right," Berry said.

"I was thinking the same thing," Raina replied. "Let's see what we can find around here."

Berry took out a magnifying glass from her bag. "I came prepared!" she said.

Raina turned and stubbed her toe on a rock sticking out of the ground. "Ouch!" she cried. She bent down to see what had stopped her. "Look at this," she said.

"You don't need a magnifying glass to see that that is a coconut!" Dash exclaimed.

"A tropical treasure," Cocoa said.

Berry examined the coconut. She carefully lifted it up. "It's almost like it has a golden shell. I have never seen anything like this."

"Um, and I have never seen anything like *that*!" Melli squealed.

Raina saw Melli's wide eyes and knew something was wrong. She looked over and saw a large purple-and-red snake!

"Holy peppermint!" Dash shouted. "That is the biggest snake I have ever seen."

"Stay away," Cocoa said. "We don't know if it's dangerous."

The fairies flew up above the ground and watched as the snake slithered around the gummy plants and headed to a sandy area by the lagoon.

"Sweet strawberries!" Berry cried. "Did you see that?"

Cocoa rubbed her eyes and nodded. "I saw it," she said. "But I don't believe it."

The snake had disappeared into the sand. "I think that must be sugar quicksand," Raina told her friends. "I read about that once, but I have never seen it."

"Does that mean the snake is gone?" Melli asked. Her wings were fluttering quickly and she was speaking very fast. Raina knew her friend was frightened.

"Don't worry, Melli," Raina said. "The snake can't fly."

Berry flew down a little closer to the ground. "This makes you wonder what else could be in that quicksand, huh?" she asked.

 21

Raina tapped her finger on her chin. "I wonder if there might be some clues about the tropical flavors in that sticky sand. The question is, how are we going to find out what is in there?"

"We need a plan," Dash said. "A supersticky sandy plan."

CHAPTER 3

Quicksand Trouble

Raina stared at the sugar quicksand pit. She thought for a moment. Then she reached for a gummy branch on the ground and threw it toward the sand. In an instant the branch sank down into the shimmering sandy pond.

"Whoa," Dash said. "That was *sugar mint*!"

"Sugar quicksand, all right," Raina said.

"Do you think there might be other things down in the quicksand?" Cocoa asked. She moved to the edge of the sandy area. "I wish we could see in there."

"Me too," Raina replied. She picked up another branch and flew over the sand pit.

"Raina!" Melli cried. "What are you going to do?"

"Careful!" Berry exclaimed.

Raina dipped the stick into the thick quicksand. It was hard to keep flying and poke around. Pulling the stick out of the sand was not easy. Each time she tugged the stick, she felt a strain in her wings. She struggled to move the stick.

"Come back over here," Cocoa told her. "It's not safe there."

Raina's wings were beginning to ache. Her friends were right to worry. A fairy's wings were not made for holding her in one place while she poked into sugar quicksand. She flew back to stand with her friends.

"Anyone have any ideas?" Raina asked. Her tired wings drooped down.

Dash shook her head. "It's never a good sign when Raina doesn't know what to do," she whispered.

"Hold on," Berry said. "Let's think about this for a minute. There has got to be a way to explore that sand pit."

Raina sat down and leaned against a gummy tree. "Maybe this is why no Candy Fairies come here anymore," she said. "This place isn't haunted. It is just plain old sticky!" She looked over at Berry.

"You know I'm going to say it," Berry said. She flew over to Raina and sat down next to her. "Don't dip your wings in syrup—or quicksand—yet. We will find a way to get to the bottom of this."

"Hot caramel!" Melli exclaimed. She pointed at the stick that was still in the quicksand. "Look at the end of the stick. It's like it has a caramel coating."

The Candy Fairies studied Raina's stick. There was a golden layer around the tip.

"*So mint!*" Dash cried.

"I guess that sugar quicksand makes a cara-mel coating," Melli said.

Dash held up the coconut Raina had found earlier. "Look, the shell has the same gold-colored coating. This must have been in the quicksand too," she said.

Raina took the coconut in her hand. Dash was right: This coconut had been in the quick-sand. But how did it get out? "This is a great sign," she said. "If this coconut got out, maybe we can fish other things out of the sand."

"A coconut clue," Berry said. "I wonder if the sugar quicksand has hidden away candy treasures for many years."

Raina hugged the coconut. "That's it, Berry!" she exclaimed. "The secret to the lost gummy flavors is hidden in that sand," she said. "And this coconut might be the answer."

"I don't even like coconut," Dash mumbled.

"Really?" Berry asked. "Finally a flavor you don't like?"

Dash gave Berry a sour look. "Very funny," she said.

"Let's try to work together," Raina said. She flew between Dash and Berry.

They heard a loud cry above in the branches, and all five fairies looked up.

"Cocoa monkeys!" Cocoa cried. "Oh, look how cute they are!"

The Candy Fairies watched the monkeys as they leaped and swung from tree to tree.

"Looks like those monkeys are bickering too," Melli said. She giggled. "Maybe Raina will have to stand between them."

"I don't think they are fighting," Cocoa said. She saw the playful monkeys jumping around on the branches. "I think they are trying to tell us something."

"Or they are just having fun swinging around," Dash added.

"I wonder if they know if more treasures are in that sand pit," Raina said.

"Someone must have pulled this coconut out of the sand," Berry told her. "Maybe these crazy cocoa monkeys can help us."

Cocoa nodded. "Cocoa monkeys definitely like coconuts," she said. "Maybe they know how to fish stuff out of the sand."

Raina saw how the monkeys grabbed on to long gummy vines and playfully tugged at one another.

"Cocoa, do you think you can talk to these monkeys?" Raina asked.

"I can try," Cocoa said. "Cocoa monkeys are not known to be the easiest animals. They like to do what they like . . . not what you ask them."

"Maybe we just need to watch them," Raina replied. She couldn't take her eyes off the little monkeys, and she noticed how easily they moved from vine to vine. "If we can see how they fish things out of the quicksand, then maybe we can too."

"That's a *sugar-tastic* idea!' Melli cried.

Raina sat down. "It will be *sugar-tastic* if it works," she said softly. "I hope these monkeys have a few tricks to share with us. Otherwise we will be going home with a flavorless story."

 30

CHAPTER 4

Mystery of Gummy Lagoon

This is one crazy cocoa monkey show," Dash said.

The Candy Fairies were sitting on a gummy tree branch, watching the monkeys swing back and forth. The monkeys took turns grabbing the licorice vines and flying over the sugar quicksand like they were performing a show at Candy Castle. These monkeys were so graceful—and brave. They reached for a vine and dangled above the sand without looking scared. Raina wondered if she could hold on to a vine like the monkeys.

Suddenly one of the monkeys grabbed a long stick and dragged it through the sand pit as he swung on the vine.

"Raina, look at that little one with the branch," Cocoa said. "He makes this look so easy."

"He's looking for something," Berry replied. "Watch!"

The small monkey's stick hit something buried in the sand. He started to squeal, and another monkey jumped on a vine to swing closer. The Candy Fairies couldn't believe their eyes: This monkey had a net! He dipped down and scooped up a coconut from the pit.

"Did you see that move?" Dash said.

"Lickin' lollipops!" Berry said. "Those are some fast-flying monkeys."

Raina noticed that the net didn't go too deep into the sand. "It looks like the sugar is so thick and gooey that the coconuts don't actually sink all the way down," she said.

"What we're looking for isn't lost," Berry said. "It's just covered."

"And what exactly are we looking for?" Dash asked.

Raina's wings drooped. "Well, I am not really sure," she said.

"You always check the Fairy Code Book for information," Melli said. "Maybe we should also check Prince Scoop's *Tropical Treasures* book."

Cocoa gave Melli a hug. "You are thinking like Raina!" she said. "That is a *choc-o-rific* idea!"

Melli picked up Prince Scoop's book. She started to flip through the pages. "Did you read all the stories in here?" she asked Raina.

"Not all of them," Raina admitted to her friends. "There aren't as many stories as in the Fairy Code Book, but I got so excited after reading the first chapter about Gummy Lagoon," she said. "I had to come here right away." She moved closer to Melli and peered over her shoulder. "I probably should have read more," she said softly.

Melli carefully turned the pages of the

old book. "We can read the stories together," she said. "Don't you always say that fairy stories help us figure out what to do?"

Raina smiled at her friend. "Thanks, Melli," she said. "You are a good friend."

"And a good reader, too," Cocoa added.

Melli stopped flipping the pages of the book. "Doesn't this look like the coconut shell we just found?" she asked.

The fairies crowded around Melli and looked at the picture she was pointing to in the book. There was a drawing of a wand with a special-looking coconut at the end. The

36

coconut had a design carved into the sides. Below the picture there was a sentence: *The flavor wand of Gummy Lagoon.*

"*Choc-o-rific,* Melli!" Cocoa gushed. "I think you just solved the mystery of the lagoon!"

"A magic gummy wand?" Raina asked. "I have never heard of such a thing."

"Maybe because it's been buried in the sugar quicksand," Dash replied.

"Sweet sugars," Raina gasped. "All these years without the tropical flavors, and the answer is here in this sandy goo?"

Melli put her hand up. "Hold on," she said. "We really should read some more of the story. You can't tell the whole story from one picture."

Raina knew that Melli was right, but her

mind was racing. What if she was able to find this wand? She started to think of all the flavors she could harvest and all the scrumptious gummy flowers she could grow. She could create a whole tropical feast of delicious fruity flavors. Princess Lolli and Prince Scoop would be so proud!

"Raina!" Berry said loudly. "Are you listening to us?"

"Sorry," Raina said softly. She had not heard a single word her friends had said since she'd seen that picture of the gummy wand.

"I said," Berry continued, "that the tip of that wand looks just like the golden coconut we found." She held up the coconut. "I rubbed off the extra sugar sand on it, and there is the same drawing." She put it next to the book so

Raina could see the markings. "We found a piece of the magic gummy wand!"

"Hot chocolate!" Cocoa exclaimed. "Look at that carving!"

"*Sugar-tastic,*" Raina said, in awe of the work. "This *must* be the tip of the magic wand."

Berry clapped her hands. "Now we just need to find the wand!"

"There are many other stories in this book," Melli said. "We should read some more. I bet there are more clues in the other stories."

"Now you *really* sound like Raina!" Dash exclaimed.

Raina stood up and fluttered her wings. "The wand might be in the quicksand, just like the coconut. I think we should try to look for it."

Melli shook her head. "But we could get stuck in that sand," she said.

Dash shuddered. "And get a thick sugar coating."

Berry flew up in the air. "Come on," she said with a burst of enthusiasm. "Let's give it a try and see what we can find."

Raina was thankful for Berry's positive attitude. "Berry's right," she said. "We at least need to try. Let's find some long branches so we can stir up the sand and poke around." She looked up at the monkeys swinging from the branches. "We are going to be like fearless cocoa monkeys," she said.

"I was afraid she was going to say that," Melli said, sighing.

"Come on, Melli," Raina said. "You found

 40

the picture. Now let's find the wand."

But before they could start, Melli grew very quiet and dropped the book onto the ground. Then she cried, "We've got company again!"

A large orange gummy alligator was crawling around the edge of the sand pit.

But instead of flying away, Raina smiled. "I think we've just got the extra help we needed," she said. She flew down to the alligator as her friends stared at her in disbelief.

5

Hagoo's Surprise

R aina!" Cocoa shouted. "What are you doing? That's an alligator!"

"And he has some large teeth!" Dash added.

Raina looked back at her friends standing on the branch above her. She waved at them. "Don't be afraid," she said. "Come down. It's fine." She landed next to the alligator. "This is

Hagoo. I've read a ton of stories about him."

"And did any of those stories say that the large alligator with the large teeth is friendly?" Berry asked. She raised her eyebrows and peered down at Hagoo.

"Yes, of course," Raina called. "Hagoo has been living here in Gummy Forest forever." She shrugged. "Well, at least for a long time."

"He's not going to be mad we're here in the lagoon?" Dash asked.

"I'll ask him," Raina said bravely. She flew over to Hagoo and hovered above him.

"Is she really speaking to an alligator?" Melli asked.

Raina saw Hagoo's kind eyes and knew that the stories of the wise, gentle alligator were true. He wouldn't hurt a Candy Fairy.

And maybe he would even help them. Raina showed Hagoo the golden coconut they had found. He slowly nodded his large head and then pointed his tail toward the sand pit.

"Thank you, Hagoo," Raina said. "Let me get my friends. I'll be right back."

Raina flew up to the other fairies. They all shared the same scared expression. She knew it was not every day a Candy Fairy saw a large gummy alligator. "I think he is telling us that the wand might be buried in the sand," Raina said. "Please come down and meet Hagoo. He really is a kind animal." She held out her hands to her friends.

"Wait," Berry said. "It looks like Hagoo is pointing to the cave near those rocks, *not* to the quicksand."

 44

The five friends flew down to Hagoo. Berry, Melli, Cocoa, and Dash kept a safe distance above the alligator.

"Berry, you're right," Raina said. "Hagoo *is* pointing to that cave."

Hagoo moved slowly toward the rocks behind the quicksand, looking back to make sure the Candy Fairies were following.

Melli flew over to get Prince Scoop's book, which she had dropped, and then followed her friends to the cave. She hugged the book close to her chest. "Are you sure about this, Raina?" she asked.

"Sure as sugar," Raina replied. "Hagoo is trying to help us. I just know it." She stood next to Hagoo at the edge of the cave and peered inside.

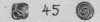

"Don't worry," Dash told them. "I came prepared." She pulled out a bunch of mint sticks from her bag. The minty glow lit up the dark cave. "There's nothing like the safety of a mint stick in a dark place," she said.

Raina took the stick from Dash. "Thank you, Dash. You are always prepared for an adventure."

"In a minty minute!" she said. "You never know when a little mint is needed."

The five fairies huddled close together as they followed Hagoo into the cave. The ground was damp and the air had a chill. Raina had the feeling that no Candy Fairy had set foot in the cave for a long time. She took a deep breath as she continued into the darkness.

"This is not quite what I had in mind when I said I would come to the lagoon," Melli said. "I was thinking of blue water and glorious flowers and reefs."

"Not to mention yummy gummy candy," Dash mumbled. She held up her mint stick. "How much farther is Hagoo going?"

Just then the alligator stopped. He turned and pointed his tail to the wall. Raina held up her mint stick, and suddenly she saw why Hagoo had taken them there. All around them were drawings on the walls of the cave.

"*So mint!*" Dash exclaimed when she saw the artwork.

"This is like a giant storybook," Melli said in awe.

"What does it all mean?" Cocoa asked.

"These look like ancient drawings," Raina told them. "And look! Each one is signed Gem the Gummy Fairy."

"Who is Gem?" Dash asked.

Raina shook her head. She ran her hand over the drawings carved into the stone. "I don't know, but imagine what Gem is trying to tell us."

"Or warn us about," Berry whispered.

Raina pulled Berry's hand. "Come on. Let's explore a little. Maybe there is a picture of the coconut wand we saw in Prince Scoop's book."

"Let's try to figure out the whole story," Melli said.

Raina fluttered her wings and gazed at the rock wall in front of her. Her mouth fell open and she felt a rush of excitement. "According to these pictures, a flavor wand does exist!" she cried. "Look!"

Carved into the stone was a picture of a wand with a coconut at the tip. It was surrounded by pieces of tropical fruit. There were drawings of pineapples, melons, papayas, and mangos. *"Sugar-tastic!"* she exclaimed.

Berry flew over to the drawing and stared at the wand. "It's beautiful," she whispered.

"And look here," Raina said, flying farther into the cave. "Here is a picture of a gum-gum bird. Why do you think there is a carving of that bird here?"

"Definitely another clue," Cocoa said. "Did anyone see a gum-gum bird when we were near the lagoon?"

"I would have remembered seeing a bird

like that," Dash said. "They are known for their flavored candies." She blushed. "I do know some things about Sugar Valley history!"

"That's right, Dash," Raina said, smiling. "And here the bird is holding the wand in her beak. It looks like the gum-gum bird took the wand and hid it."

Berry pointed at another carving and said, "The bird took the coconut off."

"The gum-gum bird hid the parts of the wand," Melli added. "I wonder why?"

Hagoo turned and crawled out of the cave. Raina motioned for the others to follow. Once they were outside, Hagoo lifted his head to the sky.

Raina was amazed at the sight. There, on a branch above, was a gum-gum bird. Her

feathers were a glossy black, with bright pink and yellow on her wing tips and chest. Her long orange and pink beak shone like the sun.

"Holy peppermint," Dash gasped.

The bird flew down and landed on Raina's arm. Raina gazed at the bird. "I bet you are here to help us," she said. She looked down at Hagoo. "Thank you," she said.

Hagoo bowed his head and crawled into the green gummy grass. The bird on Raina's arm spread her wings and took off. The five Candy Fairies flew after her, hoping this would lead to a sweet ending.

CHAPTER
6

Gum-Gum Magic

Raina flew behind the gum-gum bird with her friends. She had to work hard to keep up! The bird's wings were much larger than a fairy's wings, and the bird was flying super-fast. Raina looked over her shoulder at her friends. She knew they were all thinking the same thing: *Where is this bird taking us?*

As they flew farther away from the lagoon, Raina got nervous. Maybe she should have read Prince Scoop's book cover to cover. It wasn't like her not to finish a book. She should have known better. Was she putting her friends in danger? Her mind was whirling as fast as her wings were flapping.

"I think we can trust this gum-gum," Berry said, flying up beside Raina. "You trust Hagoo, right?"

Raina was thankful Berry was thinking that going on this journey was the right thing to do. After all, the pictures in the cave had shown a gum-gum bird with a wand in her beak. And Raina trusted Hagoo. They had to keep going if they wanted to solve this mystery.

"Do you think she is flying so fast because

no one should see us?" Cocoa asked Raina.

"Maybe," Raina said.

"Oh, thank our sugar stars!" Melli cried. "She's landed on that branch up ahead."

"I'm exhausted," Cocoa said with a heavy sigh.

Dash shot ahead. "Come on," she called. "We're at the finish line! Time to speed it up!"

"Easy for you to say," Melli said, trying to keep up with her friends.

The five fairies landed on the rim of a large nest. The strands of grass and gummy leaves that made up the nest were colorful and smelled delicious. Raina was amazed at the pattern and colors the gum-gum had selected for her home. The bird nodded to the inside ledge, and the fairies sat down.

"Oh, look!" Dash said. "She's going to feed us!"

There was a large tray of gummy candies spread out before the fairies.

"Maybe we look hungry?" Dash asked, stuffing her mouth with gummy treats.

Berry shot Dash a look. "I don't think this is all about us," she said. She turned to Raina. "What else did Prince Scoop say to you when he gave you the book? Did he mention anything about Gummy Lagoon? Or a mysterious wand?"

Raina thought back to when Prince Scoop had given her the book. She didn't remember any talk about a wand, but the cave drawings were clear. There was a coconut wand. "Maybe there were two tropical-flavor wands," Raina said, thinking out loud. "And one wand was taken to Ice Cream Isles, and the Gummy

Lagoon wand was hidden by the gum-gums."

"But why?" Melli asked. "Why did the gum-gums feel they had to hide the wand?"

"We should ask her," Dash said.

Dash was right. Raina wanted to get to the bottom of this. She was about to ask the bird, when suddenly the whole sky seemed to fill up with gum-gums. There was a lot of squawking, and the birds were swooping around the nest.

"Looks like we have some company," Berry said.

"And they don't look too happy," Dash added.

Raina looked over at the gum-gum who had brought them to the nest. She didn't look worried or alarmed at the angry birds around them.

But they were squawking so loudly!

"Maybe they are trying to warn us," Melli said.

"Or punish this bird for showing us her nest," Raina replied. She grew more and more concerned. "Let's not panic yet," she said bravely. "I think we need to remain calm."

"Easier said than done," Melli mumbled.

"She's the biggest of the gum-gums, so maybe she is the leader," Berry said, pointing to their host. "It's good that she is on our side."

The large gum-gum bird stood on the rim of her nest and squawked at the other birds. Suddenly there was quiet.

"Wow," Dash said. "She's got some magical power."

Raina stood up. "I don't know if you will understand me," she said to the birds around

the nest. "I am Raina the Gummy Fairy, and my friends and I want to bring back the tropical flavors that have been lost to Candy Kingdom." She paused and looked around at the birds. "Can you help us? This gum-gum bird has been so kind."

She wasn't sure if the birds understood her or not, but they did start to fly away. The five Candy Fairies held their breath. What were the gum-gums going to do? Did they understand?

Raina turned back to look at the gum-gum in the nest. She had a kind expression on her face and lifted up her wing. Raina moved closer to her. Now that all the gum-gums had flown away, there was silence. With her brightly colored orange-and-pink beak, the gum-gum bird pulled a silver wand from the side of the nest and dropped it into Raina's hands. Then she spread her large wings and flew off.

"I guess sometimes you just have to ask," Dash said.

"Sweet sugars, Raina," Berry told her friend, "you got the wand."

CHAPTER

7

Special Treats

Raina couldn't believe she was holding the gummy wand in her hand! It looked just like the one Gem the Gummy Fairy had drawn in the cave. Now she could bring back all those delicious, beautiful tropical tastes to Candy Kingdom. She reached into her bag for the coconut. The quicksand coating had peeled off, so now she could see the carvings on the sides much better than before.

"What is that picture on the coconut?" Berry asked. She squinted and tried to make out the drawings. "Is it a gum-gum bird?"

"I think you're right," Raina said, holding up the coconut. "I guess that is why these birds are so protective of the wand. Did you notice that the colors at the ends of their black feathers are the same as tropical flavors?"

Berry held up a stray feather from the nest. "I did," she said. "I was thinking about taking some of these stray feathers for some of my own designs."

"I'm sure you'll make something super *sugar-tastic*," Cocoa said.

"Where did our friend the gum-gum bird go?" Dash said, looking around.

Melli put her hand up to shade her eyes from the sun. She looked up at the sky. "I don't know where she went, but I think our company is back," she said.

High above the nest, the group of gum-gum birds lined up on the surrounding branches.

"Maybe they don't like that we have the wand," Cocoa said.

Raina had never seen such an angry reaction from an animal in Gummy Forest. She took care of the gummy bears, fish, and other animals.

"We'd better take cover," Melli said, looking

concerned. "Without our gum-gum friend here, we are not safe out in the open."

"Melli's right," Cocoa said. "Let's duck under these gummy vines in the nest so we can figure out what to do about these angry birds. We need to stay covered until we figure out what is going on with the gum-gums and this wand."

"We've finally got the wand and the coconut in the same place," Dash said. "Can't we see what happens when this wand is put together?"

Melli opened the *Tropical Treasures* book. She flipped through some pages. "We really need to know about the wand before we try to use it."

Raina had to admit that Melli was making

a good point. She wasn't thinking as clearly as Melli. As much as she wanted to try the wand, she knew even fairies had to be careful with something that might be magic. . . .

"With any magic, we have to be sure we're careful," Raina said. "Who knows what mischief we can make if we start waving this wand around."

"Maybe we'll get some candy," Dash muttered. "Candy with delicious tropical colors and tastes." She rubbed her stomach and licked her lips.

"Or we could get some sour magic," Cocoa said. "We should look up more stories."

Dash hung her head low. "Oh, I was afraid someone was going to say that," she said.

Raina moved some of the gummy vines

aside to make room. The five friends huddled together around the *Tropical Treasures* book. In chapter fifteen, Raina pointed to the page. "Read this!" she cried. "There were two wands in two different kingdoms!"

"So there *is* another wand in Ice Cream Isles," Melli said. "That makes sense!"

Berry took the coconut from Raina. "And if we place this coconut on the end, we solve the problem of the missing tropical gummy flavors in Candy Kingdom!"

"But why was the wand hidden in Gummy Lagoon?" Raina asked. "I think we need to know that part of the story."

The squawking gum-gums were getting louder.

"They know we're here," Dash said.

Raina flipped to the next chapter in *Tropical Treasures*. "There must be more stories in here about Gummy Lagoon," she said. "I bet there is another clue in here about why the gum-gums are so angry at us."

"Can you read faster?" Cocoa asked.

Raina looked up. The birds were getting louder. "We need to face them," she said bravely. "They must be scared. Think about it: No Candy Fairy has been here in years. We need to explain to them that we mean no harm."

"Do you think you can explain that?" Melli asked. "Did you find any reason for why the birds hid the wand?"

Raina turned the page and saw the answer

to that question. "I've got it!" she cried. "I know why the gum-gums hid the wand!"

"Good timing," Berry said, peeking out from the nest. "We are surrounded by gum-gums!"

CHAPTER 8

Gummy Secrets

Trolls!" Raina exclaimed. "There was a troll stealing candy from Gummy Lagoon!" She turned *Tropical Treasures* around to show her friends. "Look!" She tapped the picture in the book. "Her name was Guma, and she stole gummy candy—tropical-flavored gummy candy!"

"Whoa," Berry said. "Look at her. She looks bigger than Mogu!"

"I wouldn't want to meet up with her," Melli said, covering her eyes.

Raina read the passage to her friends. "Guma lived in the lagoon many years before Mogu came to Sugar Valley. She would hide out in the quicksand. The greedy troll would steal the gummy candies and leave none for the gum-gums. For years she roamed the lagoon and stole candy."

"No wonder the gum-gums don't want the wand being used again," Cocoa said. "What a terrible feeling to have your candy taken from you."

"Now I understand why the gum-gums hid the wand," Berry said. "They thought they were protecting the lagoon by stopping the tropical harvests. If there were no more gummies, then there would be no more troll."

"But hiding the wand wasn't the answer," Raina said. "We have to get the gum-gums to see that they can't be afraid of trolls. Everyone deserves to enjoy the delicious tropical flavors." She closed the book and put it back in her bag. "Those pictures in the cave showed us one solution to the problem: The gum-gums took the wand from Gem the Gummy

 74

Fairy and hid it away. But that isn't the best solution."

"I hope we can get the gum-gums to understand that we can't hide from trolls," Cocoa said.

"If we hid from trolls all the time, Sugar Valley wouldn't have any candy!" Dash exclaimed.

"Hagoo introduced us to that nice gum-gum bird," Melli said. "Where is that bird now? She would be able to speak to the others."

Berry looked out at the surrounding trees. "It would be nice to have a friend in the bunch now," she said.

"We should give them some candy," Cocoa said. "Remember what Dash said: Come prepared! We do have candy. Let's give them some."

The squawking was growing louder and

louder. More birds lined the branches of the tree where the Candy Fairies were hiding. Even though the birds couldn't see the fairies hidden in the nest, they knew they were there.

"That is worth a try," Raina said. "We need to act quickly. I hope our gum-gum friend returns soon, but in the meantime, Cocoa is right. Let's make a Candy Fairies special treat for these birds."

Raina parted the gummy vines of the nest and flew out. She waved her arms above her head. "Hello!" she said. She waited a moment and chose her words carefully. "We're Candy Fairies. We have some of our own candy to share with you."

The birds quieted down and stayed perched on the branches of the trees.

"I think they understood," Cocoa whispered.

"Actually, I don't think they are mad," Raina said. "Look at them. These sounds are cheers of happiness. These gum-gums aren't mad. They are happy!"

"And look!" Berry said, pointing. "There's Hagoo!"

The Candy Fairies flew to the edge of the nest, holding chocolates, mints, caramels, and lollipops. They flew around the tree branches and sprinkled candy over the gum-gums.

"I think they like the treats," Melli whispered to Raina. "Look how they are eating the candies. It's a celebration."

"Wait!" Raina cried. She pointed up to the northern part of the sky. "Look, our gum-gum friend is back!" she said. The bird landed on

the rim of her nest and cooed sweetly to the crowd of birds.

"What is she saying?" Cocoa asked.

"The birds wanted the Candy Fairies to come back here," Raina said, looking around. "They wanted the wand to come out of hiding too." Raina smiled at the gum-gums and waved to Hagoo crawling on the ground. "I think it's time we join the wand and the coconut together," she said.

"Finally!" Dash cried. "I can't wait!"

"Oh, I hope this works," Melli said with a heavy sigh.

"I hope we don't disappoint all these birds," Raina added. She wasn't sure what would happen once the wand was put back together.

CHAPTER
9

Tropical Burst

Cocoa held up the wand up so Raina could place the coconut on the tip. After dreaming about finding the answer to the lost flavors of Gummy Lagoon, Raina had the power in her hands. The drawings in the cave and the stories in the book all made perfect sense to her now. Finally she was given the chance to make the lagoon blossom again.

"Let's do this together," Raina said.

"Sure as sugar," Cocoa replied.

Raina took a deep breath. While Cocoa steadied the wand, she placed the coconut on the tip.

"Let's show these gum-gum birds what a tropical candy feast looks like!" Dash said.

Cocoa raised the wand up. There was complete silence as Cocoa waved the wand around.

Nothing happened.

Raina shot Cocoa a worried look. "The wand looks just like the drawings in the cave," she said, confused. "I don't understand."

"Maybe the wand isn't working," Melli said quietly. "Maybe we are too late. It has been a long time."

Raina shook her head. "Impossible," she said. "Wands don't just stop working. Cocoa, try again."

Cocoa waved the wand around again.

The gum-gums' wings began to rustle and there was soft squawking.

Nothing appeared. No tropical feast in a rainbow of colors. There was no gummy magic happening at all. Cocoa put down the wand. There was nothing to celebrate after all.

"Wait a minute," Cocoa said. "Remember my chocolate wand?" Cocoa took Raina's hand. "It only worked when *I* held it." She handed the wand to Raina. "You need to try this before we all give up hope. This wand was meant for a Gummy Fairy."

"Cocoa's right!" Berry said. "Don't give up

hope yet, Raina. Give the wand a try yourself."

Raina took the wand and closed her eyes. She felt a tingle in her fingers. The wand warmed up the instant she touched it. She opened her eyes and saw the wand start to glow.

"I think the wand is working," Dash said. She clapped her hands. "More tropical treats, please!"

The gum-gums didn't move a feather. They didn't make a peep. All the birds in the trees stood at attention as Raina the Gummy Fairy waved the coconut wand.

And sure as sugar, there was a different result when Raina waved the wand.

All around them, plants sprouted up, trees became fuller, and flowers began to bloom. A burst of colors covered the area, and a sweet scent of tropical fruit filled the air.

There was squawking again: The birds were celebrating!

"Raina!" Melli cried. "You did it!"

"There is magic in the wand!" Berry said. She hugged Raina tightly. "We needed a Gummy Fairy's touch. You brought the magic back to Gummy Lagoon."

"We all brought the magic back," Raina told her. She flew over to the gum-gum bird who had showed her kindness. "Thank you for believing in me and my friends," she said. She wasn't sure if the bird understood, but the bird cooed softly. "Fairy promise that we will help protect you from Mogu or any other troll who wanders through here."

The gum-gum bird spread her wings and

let out a deep sigh. She shook some nearby branches and a shower of brand-new candies fell into her nest.

The colors of the candies were not familiar to Raina or her friends. She knew at once these must be the lost flavors, and she was so excited to try the candies. She smiled at the gum-gum bird and picked up a pale yellow gummy. Holding the candy in her hand, she tried to imagine what flavor the candy would be.

When a burst of pineapple filled her mouth, she grinned. "Supersweet!" she said. She turned to her friends. "You must try these!"

"Mango!" Dash said as she popped a pale orange treat into her mouth. "I want to try every color and shape! I could spend all day here!"

 85

"Coconut!" Cocoa cried. She licked her fingers after trying a white gummy candy.

Berry and Melli reached for gummies sprinkled in the nest. Their faces lit up when they tasted the candies.

"Lickin' lollipops!" Berry exclaimed. "This is delicious."

"And look, the cocoa monkeys are munching on those gummy bananas growing on the trees!" Dash said. "I need to try those too!" She flew off to pick one of the new gummy candies from the tree in front of her.

"Better than I imagined," Melli said, after eating a mango-flavored flower. "Wait till Princess Lolli and Prince Scoop see all this. They won't believe their eyes."

"Let's send a sugar fly right away," Raina

said. She waved down a messenger and sent a quick note to Candy Castle. "They have to see all this. What a sight this place is now!"

The gum-gum bird sat back in her nest, cooing happily. Raina flew to her side.

"Guma is long gone," Raina told her. "There might be other trolls to watch out for, but we will look after you and the others. These treats should be for all the fairies and animals in Sugar Valley."

The gum-gum bird nodded. All around them, a celebration continued. Gum-gum birds were singing happily, and Hagoo raised his head proudly. Raina saw that the old alligator was pleased. Once again the lagoon was filled with brightly colored candies. No longer was the area dull and barren.

"Thank you, Hagoo," Raina said, flying down to the alligator. "Without you, this would not have happened."

Hagoo bowed his head. He seemed very pleased. Raina threw her arms around the orange alligator and gave a tight squeeze. "I will never forget how brave and smart you were today."

"Did you see all the gummies on these branches?" Dash said, flying over to Raina and Hagoo. "Or on those vines over there?"

Raina laughed. There was something to look at all around them. She was so glad that Gummy Lagoon would once again be a place where Candy Fairies and gummy animals could harvest and enjoy candy.

Now they just needed to keep the gum-

gums and their candy supply safe from trolls. As the celebration continued around her, Raina was thinking of a plan to keep trolls out of Gummy Lagoon. Once Mogu heard of the return of the tropical gummy candy, he was sure to show up.

Raina had to think of a plan. She had made a fairy promise and had to keep it.

CHAPTER 10

Sweet Endings

Raina signaled to her friends. The five fairies huddled together on a branch near the nest.

"We need to come up with a plan to help the gum-gums feel safe," Raina said. She was trying to keep her voice low, but the celebration going on around them made that difficult. She didn't want to upset the birds and the monkeys. Raina wanted them to enjoy the happy moment. But she also wanted to be prepared.

"I hope Mogu is not on his way here now," Melli said. "He will want to see what all the fuss is about."

"Exactly what I was thinking," Raina said. She watched the scene down below the tree. The cocoa monkeys and the gum-gum birds were so happy . . . and making a huge amount of noise.

"When he sees what is going on here, he is going to want to stay!" Dash said.

"He won't be able to resist all this new candy," Berry added.

"Who could blame him?" Dash asked, popping more gummies into her mouth. "These treats not only look good, they are good! He is going to want to have some himself."

Raina thought about what Dash had just said. And if Raina had meant it that the tropical candy should be for everyone in Sugar Valley, she had to include Mogu as well. "Mogu is welcome to some candy, but not all the candy," she said. "A troll's greed is what started all this, and now that we have the wand back, we have to be careful."

"How are you going to stop Mogu?" Melli asked.

"He is definitely not known for stopping his candy stealing," Cocoa added.

"If he takes more than his share, he won't be allowed back," Raina said firmly. "That rule is the same for everyone throughout Sugar Valley."

Dash rolled her eyes. "Funny how he forgets that rule," she said.

"We can't punish him before he does something wrong," Raina told her.

Melli fluttered her wings. "Just like we thought! Here he comes!" she said. She pointed down below, near the lagoon. "I knew his nose would sniff these fresh flavors out!"

As expected, the hungry troll was curious about all the new scents and had come to see what all the fuss was about. From the tree branch, the Candy Fairies saw Mogu slowly making his way toward them. His shirt was stained with chocolate, and his large belly hung over his short pants. A line of Chuchies followed him as he stomped through the gummy grass.

"Let's go talk to him," Raina said. She swooped down before her friends could stop her. She flew right up to the troll. She wasn't afraid. She had a message to deliver. "Mogu, you can try these candies, but you can't have them all," she said.

Mogu didn't move. He was still for a moment. He grumbled a bit as the Chuchies scattered around to collect fallen candies.

"Is he going to listen?" Berry asked.

"He'd better if he wants to stay," a voice called from above.

Raina looked up to see Princess Lolli and Prince Scoop right above them.

"We got your sugar fly message," Prince Scoop told Raina, "and we had to come right away to see the work you've done here."

Princess Lolli flew down to stand next to the Candy Fairies. "Hello, Mogu," she said.

Mogu grunted and stomped over to the lagoon, where a long vine was full of colorful bunches of gummy berries.

"Remember, these candies are for everyone, Mogu," Princess Lolli said. She turned to Raina. "You and your friends were not only brave, but smart. How did you ever find the lost wand? Many Candy Fairies have searched for the wand and have never found it."

The gum-gum bird flew down and landed on Raina's shoulder.

"I see you've met Sweets," the princess said.

"Is that your name?" Raina said, facing the bird.

Princess Lolli laughed. "Sweets is the leader of the gum-gums and the keeper of the wand. For a long time she did not trust any Candy Fairy to protect the gum-gums from the trolls who might come to take their candies here in the lagoon."

"I think Hagoo had a part in making Sweets trust us," Raina said. "I know Hagoo from my travels through Gummy Forest. He put in a good word for us."

"Yes, but *you* gained Sweets's trust," Prince Scoop told her. "Well done, Raina."

"You have saved the day!" Princess Lolli said, hugging Raina. "The wand will be kept at Candy Castle. This is a treasure that has been lost to Candy Fairies for far too long. We can keep the wand safe if it is at the castle." She smiled at Raina. "But you are more than welcome to use the wand when you need to," she said. "We want to make sure Gummy Lagoon remains this *sweet-tacular.*"

"Thank you for making this area of Gummy Forest alive again," Prince Scoop added. "I had been missing my tropical-flavored ice cream, and now we can all enjoy those flavors in candies here in Candy Kingdom."

"Please come to the castle at Sun Dip tonight,"

Princess Lolli said. "I would like to have a special dinner." She looked over at Sweets. "Please come too, Sweets. It would be an honor to have you as well."

Sweets bowed her head and squawked her happy reply.

"Don't worry about Mogu," Princess Lolli said. "We've got our eye on him. You all go ahead and get ready for dinner. We'll see you later."

The Candy Fairies hugged Princess Lolli and got ready to fly back home to change for dinner at the castle. Before she left, Raina spoke softly to Sweets. "Sweets, now that I know your name, I want to use it!" She smiled. "Even though we don't speak the same language, you trusted me, and I will not let you down. I promise to check in on you and all the gum-gums. You can count on me."

Sweets nuzzled her head into Raina's shoulder. Raina knew she had made a sweet and true new friend.

The Candy Fairies each went home to change for their royal dinner. There was great excitement throughout the kingdom as word spread about the five brave Candy Fairies who had found the missing coconut wand and made Gummy Lagoon bloom again.

Berry made special feather headpieces for all the Candy Fairies to wear to the dinner, in honor of the wand's return.

"Those feathers are extraordinary," Prince Scoop said. "You look *gummy-licious*! And now everyone in the kingdom can enjoy tropical

flavors. You have uncovered a great story and some very special treats."

The fairies blushed and took their seats at the banquet table. Sweets perched on Raina's shoulder.

Sweets cooed happily throughout the dinner. Raina knew that she and all the gum-gums would be good friends—and everyone throughout the kingdom would be sure to enjoy tropical gummy treats.

Raina took the *Tropical Treasures* book out of her bag and handed it to Prince Scoop. "Thank you for this treasure," she said, smiling. "This book proved to be a very good story for all the Candy Fairies."

Prince Scoop looked around at all the happy faces. "These new flavors are being enjoyed by so many fairies now," he said, "thanks to you and your friends. This is a great treat." He plucked a coconut gummy flower from a platter on the table. "And this is a *sweet-tastic* way to celebrate the return of the lost coconut wand!"

Raina laughed, taking a gummy flower for herself. "A very sweet ending *and* beginning filled with new flavors to try!"

FIND OUT

WHAT HAPPENS IN

Rock Candy Treasure

Melli the Caramel Fairy stood by the hot stones to melt her caramel in a clearing by Caramel Hills. She loved the sounds of Chocolate River rushing down the steep rocks. Chocolate Falls was one of her favorite places in Sugar Valley.

As she watched her pot of melting caramel

dipping sauce, she hummed. She was learning to play a new song on her licorice stick, and she couldn't get the melody out of her head. The song was hard to play, but she wanted to perform it at Candy Castle for Princess Lolli and Prince Scoop. The royal couple was hosting a dinner and had asked some Candy Fairies to play their musical instruments for the entertainment. It was a big honor, and Melli wanted her song to be perfect.

Out of the corner of her eye, Melli saw a bright streak of red and purple. She knew there were no caramel animals with those bright colors.

"Is someone there?" Melli called out. "Hello?"

A branch snapped in the woods, and Melli's heart beat faster.

"Who is hiding in there?" she asked. She had a bad feeling that maybe one of Mogu's Chuchies was hiding in the bushes. Sometimes Mogu the troll would send his little Chuchies to steal candy from Candy Fairies. Or worse than Chuchies, maybe it was Mogu!

Melli wished her other Candy Fairy friends were with her. If Cocoa the Chocolate Fairy were here, she would be brave and strong. Dash the Mint Fairy would be superfast and clever, and Raina the Gummy Fairy would be smart and know a story in the Fairy Code Book that would help. Her friend Berry the Fruit Fairy would likely not be scared at all!

"Hello?" Melli said again. Her voice sounded shaky and unsure.

The leaves on the bush in front of her

moved, and Melli grew more nervous. She tried to think brave thoughts.

"Mogu?" she asked.

"Who's Mogu?" a tiny voice said.

Melli was surprised to hear that reply. Who lived in Sugar Valley and didn't know the greedy, salty troll Mogu, who stole candy and lived in Black Licorice Swamp?

"Who are you?" Melli asked. She fluttered her wings nervously and lifted herself off the ground.

"I'm Crystal," the voice said. "But you can call me Taly. Everybody calls me Taly."

Melli knelt down on the ground where the voice was coming from. Whoever was speaking was small and seemed friendly. Melli peered between the branches. "Hello, Taly," she said. "I am Melli, a Caramel Candy Fairy."

"Are you a friendly Candy Fairy?" Taly asked.

"Of course!" Melli exclaimed. She saw the tips of tiny, bright candy-apple-red boots.

"I've never seen a Candy Fairy," Taly replied. She stepped from behind the branches and out of hiding.

Melli didn't mean to stare, but she couldn't take her eyes off the little creature. Taly had a long, pointed head and a red-and-purple-striped hat. Her dress was purple with red-and-white polka dots.

"Are you . . . a gnome?" she asked.

"Yes, I am. Do you like gnomes?" Taly asked.

Melli laughed. "I've never met a gnome," she said. "My friend Raina once read me a fairy tale about a gnome named Gumbu, but I have never met one."

"I don't know Gumbu," Taly said. She moved closer to Melli and peered behind her back. "Can you fly?" she asked, looking at Melli's wings.

Melli fluttered her wings. "Yes, I can," she said. "See?" She lifted herself up in the air.

Taly's eyes opened very wide. She looked around at Caramel Hills. "Where am I?"

"This is Caramel Hills," Melli told her. "I live here with other Caramel Fairies."

Taly raised her head and took a big sniff. "What is that smell?" she asked.

"Sweet sugars!" Melli cried. "That is my caramel burning!" She flew over to the hot stones and lifted the pot of bubbling caramel off the hook. "Oh no," she said, peering inside the pot at her burnt caramel.

"Is it ruined?" Taly asked.

Melli stirred the pot. "I think so," she said. She shook her head. "That is not like me at all."

"It's my fault," Taly said. "I'm sorry." The little gnome's eyes filled with tears.

Melli felt terrible that she had made Taly cry. "Don't worry," she said. "There is plenty more caramel. Would you like something to drink?"

Taly nodded.

"Here," Melli said, giving Taly a cup of fruit nectar. "Drink this, and you can try these caramel squares I made this morning." She reached for her basket of candy on a nearby rock.

"Thank you," Taly said. She ate everything that Melli gave her.

"You haven't eaten in a while, huh?" Melli asked. "Where did you come from, anyway?"

Taly hung her head. "I'm lost," she said quietly. "I'm not supposed to leave the caves, but needed to find something to fix our carts!"

"Caves?" Melli asked. "Carts?"

Taly pointed to Chocolate Falls. "Rock Candy Caves," she said. "We use small carts when we mine sugar from the caves."

Melli had no idea what the little gnome was talking about. She had flown around the Chocolate Falls many times, and she had never known there were caves . . . with gnomes living there! "You live in caves behind the waterfall?" she asked. "And you mine sugar?"

Taly's small hands flew up to her mouth. "I'm not supposed to tell anyone that!" she said. "Where gnomes live is a secret." She grabbed Melli's hand. "Please promise not to tell anyone."

"Sure as sugar," Melli said. She watched the little gnome eat her treat. "Will you help me get back home?" Taly asked.

"Fairy's promise," Melli replied quickly. She had to help the little gnome!

As Taly grinned and enjoyed her snack, Melli wondered if she had just made a promise that she would be able to keep!

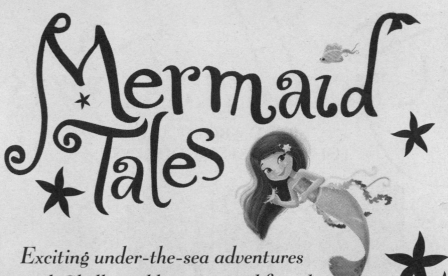

Mermaid Tales

Exciting under-the-sea adventures
with Shelly and her mermaid friends!

Trouble at Trident Academy • Battle of the Best Friends • A Whale of a Tale • Danger in the Deep Blue Sea • The Lost Princess

The Secret Sea Horse • Dream of the Blue Turtle • Treasure in Trident City • A Royal Tea • A Tale of Two Sisters

Goddess Girls

READ ABOUT ALL
YOUR FAVORITE GODDESSES!

**#17 AMPHITRITE
THE BUBBLY**

**#16 MEDUSA
THE RICH**

**#15 APHRODITE
THE FAIR**

**#14 IRIS
THE COLORFUL**

**#13 ATHENA
THE PROUD**

**#12 CASSANDRA
THE LUCKY**

**#11 PERSEPHONE
THE DARING**

**#10 PHEME
THE GOSSIP**

**#1 ATHENA
THE BRAIN**

**#2 PERSEPHONE
THE PHONY**

**#3 APHRODITE
THE BEAUTY**

**#4 ARTEMIS
THE BRAVE**

**#5 ATHENA
THE WISE**

**#6 APHRODITE
THE DIVA**

**#7 ARTEMIS
THE LOYAL**

**THE GIRL GAMES:
SUPER SPECIAL**

**#8 MEDUSA
THE MEAN**

**#9 PANDORA
THE CURIOUS**

EBOOK EDITIONS ALSO AVAILABLE
From Aladdin
KIDS.SimonandSchuster.com

Sparkle Spa

Making friends one Sparkly nail at a time!

All That Glitters

Purple Nails and Puppy Tails

Makeover Magic

True Colors

Bad News Nails

A Picture-Perfect Mess

Bring It On!

Enjoy these sweet treats from Aladdin.

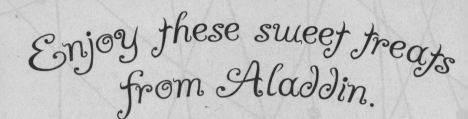

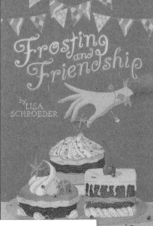

FROM ALADDIN

KIDS.SimonandSchuster.com • EBOOK EDITIONS ALSO AVAILABLE